THIS JOURNAL BELONGS TO:

Harry Potter™

AMBITION

A GUIDED JOURNAL FOR
EMBRACING YOUR INNER

SLYTHERIN™

INSIGHT
EDITIONS

San Rafael • Los Angeles • London

INTRODUCTION

AMBITIOUS. CUNNING. LEADERS BY NATURE. These are the traits of Slytherin house, the proudest house at Hogwarts, draped in their rich colors of green and silver and represented by a coiled serpent. There are many notable and beloved Slytherin characters in the Harry Potter films. From Severus Snape and Draco Malfoy to the deranged Bellatrix Lestrange, Slytherins are represented by a wide range of witches and wizards. But what does it mean to truly be a Slytherin? How can you bring out your natural qualities of ambition, cunning, and leadership and apply them to your everyday life?

This journal, composed of 52 weeks of prompts, will help you reflect on, connect with, and develop the Slytherin inside you. Each week includes two kinds of prompts. The first is a simple form where you can record daily acts of ambition, cunning, and leadership. Taking the structure of a simple "one-line-a-day" journal, this form allows you to record small "Slytherin moments" that you encounter throughout your week. There is no pressure to fill one out every day. After all, you might not have the opportunity to demonstrate leadership every day. But it gives you an opportunity to notice and note small ways that you embody your Slytherin persona. The second prompt goes deeper, referencing specific quotes, moments, places, or characters from the films and inviting you to think about how being a Slytherin shapes and affects your life. These prompts include freewriting, letter writing, list making, coloring, and more.

The Harry Potter films have inspired us, now it's time to explore further and embrace your inner Slytherin.

WEEK 1

SLYTHERIN MOMENTS:
Daily Acts of Ambition, Cunning, and Leadership

Monday

Tuesday

Wednesday

Thursday

Friday

Saturday

Sunday

WEEK 1

SLYTHERINS, LIKE DRACO MALFOY, SEVERUS SNAPE, and Horace Slughorn, rely on their cunning, ambition, and natural ability to lead to accomplish their goals. By purposefully embracing your inner Slytherin qualities, you are taking active steps to realize your dreams. What are you hoping to achieve or discover by using this journal? How do you see your Slytherin qualities helping you do this?

WEEK 2

Monday

Tuesday

Wednesday

Thursday

Friday

Saturday

Sunday

WEEK 2

COLORING MEDITATIONS

The Sorting Hat sorts each Hogwarts student into their house on
their first night at school, taking into account their background,
talents, personalities, and personal choice. Due to your ambition,
cunning, and leadership, you have been sorted into Slytherin. Color
in the hat below, and decorate the rest of the page with iconography
and embellishments that represent your identity as a Slytherin.

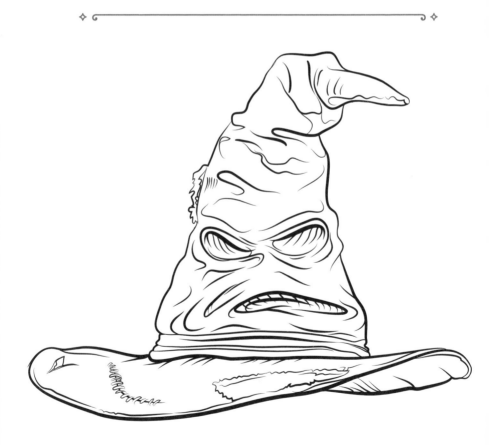

WEEK 3

SLYTHERIN MOMENTS:

Daily Acts of Ambition, Cunning, and Leadership

Monday

Tuesday

Wednesday

Thursday

Friday

Saturday

Sunday

WEEK 3

IN *HARRY POTTER AND THE SORCERER'S STONE*, Harry discovers the Mirror of Erised in an unused classroom at Hogwarts. When he looks into it, he sees his parents. As Professor Dumbledore later explains, the mirror shows the viewer whatever their heart most desires. What do you think you would see if you looked in the mirror? Do you see a connection to your identity as a Slytherin? What is it?

WEEK 4

SLYTHERIN MOMENTS:

Daily Acts of Ambition, Cunning, and Leadership

Monday

Tuesday

Wednesday

Thursday

Friday

Saturday

Sunday

WEEK 4

THERE ARE MANY AMAZING Slytherin characters in the Harry Potter films. Who is your favorite? In what way do you think this character embodies the traits of the house?

WEEK 5

SLYTHERIN MOMENTS:

Daily Acts of Ambition, Cunning, and Leadership

Monday

Tuesday

Wednesday

Thursday

Friday

Saturday

Sunday

WEEK 5

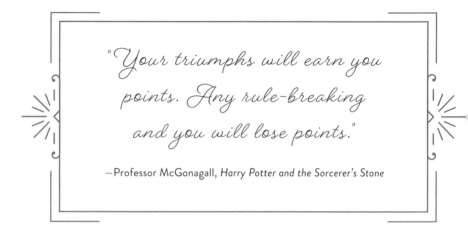

"*Your triumphs will earn you points. Any rule-breaking and you will lose points.*"

—Professor McGonagall, *Harry Potter and the Sorcerer's Stone*

It's important to celebrate our victories.

Make a list of five recent accomplishments you achieved that you believe would earn you points for Slytherin. Award yourself with the number of points you think you earned. Good job!

1. _____

_____

_____

_____ *Points:* _____

2. _____

_____

_____

_____ *Points:* _____

3. _____

_____

_____

_____ *Points:* _____

4. _____

_____

_____

_____ *Points:* _____

5. _____

_____

_____

_____ *Points:* _____

WEEK 6

SLYTHERIN MOMENTS:
Daily Acts of Ambition, Cunning, and Leadership

Monday

Tuesday

Wednesday

Thursday

Friday

Saturday

Sunday

WEEK 6

ON HARRY'S FIRST DAY AT HOGWARTS, he and Ron get lost and are late to class. As a Slytherin, imagine how you would spend your first day at Hogwarts.

WEEK 7

SLYTHERIN MOMENTS:

Daily Acts of Ambition, Cunning, and Leadership

Monday

Tuesday

Wednesday

Thursday

Friday

Saturday

Sunday

WEEK 7

OUR SKILLS AND TALENTS OFTEN reflect the inner qualities we naturally possess. For example, Harry is a skilled flier, a talent that could be said to reflect the Gryffindor traits of daringness and nerve. What specific skills and talents do you possess, and how do you feel they relate to your qualities as a Slytherin?

ABOVE: Concept art of Harry and the Firebolt by Dermot Power.

THIS PAGE: Concept art by Adam Brockbank.

WEEK 8

SLYTHERIN MOMENTS:

Daily Acts of Ambition, Cunning, and Leadership

Monday

Tuesday

Wednesday

Thursday

Friday

Saturday

Sunday

WEEK 8

PROFESSOR SNAPE is the head of Slytherin house during Harry's first few years at Hogwarts. There is no question that teachers, particularly those we work closely with, have a huge effect on the kind of person we grow up to be. Write a letter to your "head of house"—a teacher or mentor who helped you develop your Slytherin qualities—reflecting on what they taught you and thanking them for being part of your journey.

WEEK 9

SLYTHERIN MOMENTS:

Daily Acts of Ambition, Cunning, and Leadership

Monday

Tuesday

Wednesday

Thursday

Friday

Saturday

Sunday

WEEK 9

During Harry's sixth year at Hogwarts, Professor Horace Slughorn, a former head of Slytherin house, becomes the new Potions Master at Hogwarts. Professor Slughorn has a distinct teaching style. How do you think Professor Slughorn's qualities as a Slytherin are represented in his personality as a teacher? What do you think you could learn from him, both as a Slytherin and as a person?

WEEK 10

SLYTHERIN MOMENTS:

Daily Acts of Ambition, Cunning, and Leadership

Monday

Tuesday

Wednesday

Thursday

Friday

Saturday

Sunday

WEEK 10

> *"We've all got both light and dark inside us. What matters is the part we choose to act on. That's who we really are."*
>
> —Sirius Black, *Harry Potter and the Order of the Phoenix*

Sirius Black speaks this powerful quote to Harry in *Harry Potter and the Order of the Phoenix* at a moment when Harry is feeling scared, anxious, and insecure in his identity. This quote could be interpreted to mean that we all have our strong points and our weak points, our positive attributes and our flaws. Slytherins are usually described as ambitious, cunning, and resourceful. But they also have a reputation for pride and intolerance. Think about two moments in your life, one when your behavior reflected the "light" side of Slytherin and one when it reflected the "dark" side. Describe these events below. What can you learn from them?

Light: _____

_____

_____

_____

_____

_____

_____

_____

_____

_____

_____

Dark: _____

_____

_____

_____

_____

_____

_____

_____

_____

_____

_____

_____

WEEK 11

SLYTHERIN MOMENTS:

Daily Acts of Ambition, Cunning, and Leadership

Monday

Tuesday

Wednesday

Thursday

Friday

Saturday

Sunday

WEEK 11

IN *HARRY POTTER AND THE HALF-BLOOD PRINCE*, Draco Malfoy becomes a Death Eater. He spends the entire year working tirelessly and desperately to mend the Vanishing Cabinet in the Room of Requirement under Lord Voldemort's orders. Finally, at the end of the year, he succeeds. Write down three long-term goals you are currently working on. How do you see your assets as a Slytherin helping you accomplish these aspirations?

1. _____

_____

_____

2. _____

_____

_____

3. _____

_____

_____

_____

WEEK 12

SLYTHERIN MOMENTS:

Daily Acts of Ambition, Cunning, and Leadership

Monday

Tuesday

Wednesday

Thursday

Friday

Saturday

Sunday

WEEK 12

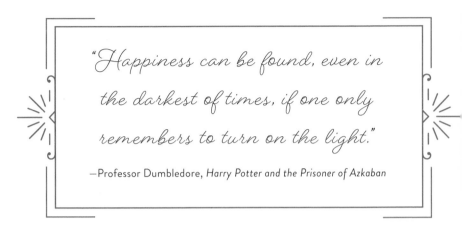

"*Happiness can be found, even in the darkest of times, if one only remembers to turn on the light.*"

—Professor Dumbledore, *Harry Potter and the Prisoner of Azkaban*

List ten things that bring joy to your Slytherin heart.

Refer back to these when you are experiencing times of trouble or stress.

1. _____

_____

2. _____

_____

3. _____

_____

4. _____

_____

5. _____
_____
_____

6. _____
_____
_____

7. _____
_____
_____

8. _____
_____
_____

9. _____
_____
_____

10. _____
_____
_____

WEEK 13

SLYTHERIN MOMENTS:

Daily Acts of Ambition, Cunning, and Leadership

Monday

Tuesday

Wednesday

Thursday

Friday

Saturday

Sunday

WEEK 13

IN *HARRY POTTER AND THE DEATHLY HALLOWS – PART 1*, Harry and his friends are captured and brought to Malfoy Manor. When Draco is asked to identify Harry, who has been disguised by a Stinging Jinx, he hedges and avoids giving a definite answer, despite the fact that, as Harry later points out, he knows perfectly well who Harry is. Do you think Draco made the right decision in that moment? Knowing what he knew at the time, would you have made the same choice? Why or why not?

WEEK 14

SLYTHERIN MOMENTS:
Daily Acts of Ambition, Cunning, and Leadership

Monday

Tuesday

Wednesday

Thursday

Friday

Saturday

Sunday

WEEK 14

COLORING MEDITATIONS

It's time to show some house pride. Color the Slytherin crest below, and decorate the rest of the page with embellishments and decorations of your choosing.

WEEK 15

SLYTHERIN MOMENTS:

Daily Acts of Ambition, Cunning, and Leadership

Monday

Tuesday

Wednesday

Thursday

Friday

Saturday

Sunday

WEEK 15

IN THE HARRY POTTER FILMS, Harry Potter and Draco Malfoy are bitter rivals. Have you ever had a rivalry with another person? Were they in the same house as you or a different one? What about this person clashed with your traits as a Slytherin?

WEEK 16

SLYTHERIN MOMENTS:

Daily Acts of Ambition, Cunning, and Leadership

Monday

Tuesday

Wednesday

Thursday

Friday

Saturday

Sunday

WEEK 16

HOGWARTS CASTLE IS A MASSIVE, ancient building filled with classrooms, student living spaces, soaring bridges, deep dungeons, high towers, moving staircases, and more than one secret room. Which aspect of the castle would you be most eager to explore? Do you see a connection between this choice and your identity as a Slytherin? How so?

THIS PAGE: Concept art of the exterior and interior of Hogwarts castle by Andrew Williamson.

CLOCKWISE FROM TOP LEFT: The exterior of Hogwarts castle by Andrew Williamson; a concept piece of the stained glass window in the prefects' bathroom by Adam Brockbank; a study of the Owlery by Andrew Williamson; a concept sketch of the second-years in Greenhouse Three by Andrew Williamson.

WEEK 17

SLYTHERIN MOMENTS:

Daily Acts of Ambition, Cunning, and Leadership

Monday

Tuesday

Wednesday

Thursday

Friday

Saturday

Sunday

WEEK 17

IMAGINE YOU HAVE THE OPPORTUNITY to interview one
Slytherin from the Harry Potter films. Who would you choose?
Write ten questions you would ask them.

10 QUESTIONS FOR: _____

1. _____

_____

_____

2. _____

_____

_____

3. _____

_____

_____

4. _____

_____

_____

WEEK 18

Monday

Tuesday

Wednesday

Thursday

Friday

Saturday

Sunday

WEEK 18

IN *HARRY POTTER AND THE HALF-BLOOD PRINCE*,
Harry retrieves a locket that he believes to be a Horcrux from the
Crystal Cave, only to discover that it is a fake, swapped out by
someone bearing the initials R.A.B. He later learns it is Regulus Black,
Sirius's brother, a Death Eater and Slytherin who ultimately betrayed
Voldemort in an attempt to destroy the Horcrux—a decision which
led to his death. Have you ever made a choice that went against your
house's traits? Why? Describe the circumstances below.

WEEK 19

SLYTHERIN MOMENTS:

Daily Acts of Ambition, Cunning, and Leadership

Monday

Tuesday

Wednesday

Thursday

Friday

Saturday

Sunday

WEEK 19

IN THE HARRY POTTER FILMS, family members are often—but not always—placed in the same houses. While all of the Weasleys are in Gryffindor and all of the Malfoys are in Slytherin, characters like Sirius Black and Parvati and Padma Patil are placed in different houses than other members of their family. What houses would your parents and siblings belong to and why? How do you think this might have contributed to your being a Slytherin?

WEEK 20

Monday

Tuesday

Wednesday

Thursday

Friday

Saturday

Sunday

WEEK 20

> "*Words are, in my not-so-humble opinion, our most inexhaustible source of magic. Capable of both inflicting injury and remedying it.*"
>
> —Professor Dumbledore, *Harry Potter and the Deathly Hallows - Part 2*

WORDS MATTER!

Write a mantra to help you tap into your inner Slytherin.

Use the space below to sketch out your thoughts, and write the final version in the shield on the next page.

MY SLYTHERIN MANTRA

WEEK 21

SLYTHERIN MOMENTS:

Daily Acts of Ambition, Cunning, and Leadership

Monday

Tuesday

Wednesday

Thursday

Friday

Saturday

Sunday

WEEK 21

"Welcome to Hogwarts. Now in a few moments, you will pass through the doors and join your classmates, but before you can take your seats, you must be sorted into your houses. They are Gryffindor, Hufflepuff, Ravenclaw, and Slytherin. Now while you're here, your house will be like your family."

—Professor McGonagall, *Harry Potter and the Sorcerer's Stone*

Think about your closest friends.

What houses do they belong to? Are they the same as you?

How does this affect your relationships?

WEEK 22

SLYTHERIN MOMENTS:

Daily Acts of Ambition, Cunning, and Leadership

Monday

Tuesday

Wednesday

Thursday

Friday

Saturday

Sunday

WEEK 22

THINK ABOUT YOUR OWN SOCIAL INTERACTIONS
as a "typical" Slytherin. Write about a time you and your friends
acted like Slytherins. What did you do? Why is this particular memory
valuable to you?

WEEK 23

SLYTHERIN MOMENTS:

Daily Acts of Ambition, Cunning, and Leadership

Monday

Tuesday

Wednesday

Thursday

Friday

Saturday

Sunday

WEEK 23

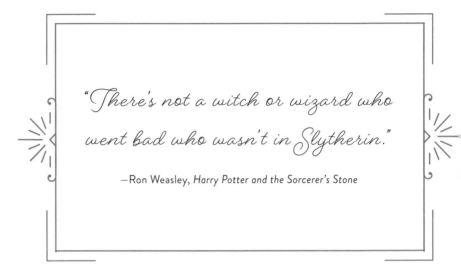

"There's not a witch or wizard who went bad who wasn't in Slytherin."

—Ron Weasley, *Harry Potter and the Sorcerer's Stone*

The above quote, spoken by Ron Weasley during the Sorting Ceremony in *Harry Potter and the Sorcerer's Stone*, illustrates the fact that stereotypes exist even in the wizarding world. Whether it's the belief that all Gryffindors are "show-offs," all Ravenclaws are "eccentric," or all Slytherins are "bad," these stereotypes can be hurtful and unfair. What are some general stereotypes about Slytherins that you feel are unfair? What do you say when confronted by them?

WEEK 24

SLYTHERIN MOMENTS:

Daily Acts of Ambition, Cunning, and Leadership

Monday

Tuesday

Wednesday

Thursday

Friday

Saturday

Sunday

WEEK 24

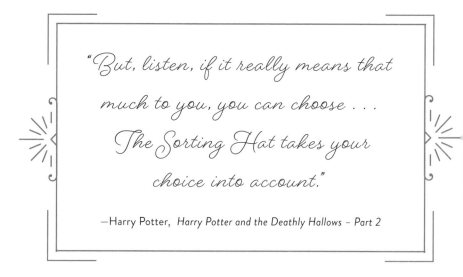

"But, listen, if it really means that much to you, you can choose . . . The Sorting Hat takes your choice into account."

—Harry Potter, *Harry Potter and the Deathly Hallows – Part 2*

In the Harry Potter films, the Sorting Hat was originally planning to put Harry in Slytherin, but he pleaded with the hat not to, and the Sorting Hat accepted his choice. Given the choice, would you choose to be in Slytherin? Why or why not?

WEEK 25

SLYTHERIN MOMENTS:

Daily Acts of Ambition, Cunning, and Leadership

Monday

Tuesday

Wednesday

Thursday

Friday

Saturday

Sunday

WEEK 25

IN *HARRY POTTER AND THE SORCERER'S STONE*, Harry, Ron, Hermione, and Draco Malfoy are caught out of bed at night and sentenced to detention in the Forbidden Forest. Imagine you've been sentenced to detention at Hogwarts. Based on your personality as a Slytherin, what rules do you think you'd be most likely to break and why?

WEEK 26

SLYTHERIN MOMENTS:

Daily Acts of Ambition, Cunning, and Leadership

Monday

Tuesday

Wednesday

Thursday

Friday

Saturday

Sunday

WEEK 26

IN *HARRY POTTER AND THE PRISONER OF AZKABAN,*
Professor Lupin teaches the third-year students how to repel a Boggart, a
Dark creature that takes the form of whatever the person fears the most.
Do you have any specific fears that relate to your identity as a Slytherin?
Fear of failure? Fear of embarrassment? Fear of snakes? Write these down
below. On the following page where it says "Riddikulus!" write what you
would use to repel the Boggart if it turned into what you fear.

ABOVE: The Boggart version of Potions Master Severus Snape, dressed as Neville Longbottom's
grandmother. Design by Jany Temime, drawn by Laurent Guinci.

Riddikulus!

ABOVE: Concept art of the jack-in-the-box version of the Boggart by Rob Bliss.

WEEK 27

SLYTHERIN MOMENTS:

Daily Acts of Ambition, Cunning, and Leadership

Monday

Tuesday

Wednesday

Thursday

Friday

Saturday

Sunday

WEEK 27

THINK ABOUT THE HOUSE you find most difficult to relate to. What is it about that house that you, as a Slytherin, find difficult to understand or appreciate?

WEEK 28

SLYTHERIN MOMENTS:
Daily Acts of Ambition, Cunning, and Leadership

Monday

Tuesday

Wednesday

Thursday

Friday

Saturday

Sunday

WEEK 28

THE SLYTHERIN COMMON ROOM is an elegantly decorated room with rich furnishings and dim, watery light, suitable for a room that is located underground and for a house that prides itself on its ancient history and strong leadership. Look around your own living space. What items or elements do you feel reflect your tastes as a Slytherin?

WEEK 29

Monday

Tuesday

Wednesday

Thursday

Friday

Saturday

Sunday

WEEK 29

THE HARRY POTTER FILMS ARE FILLED with examples of romantic pairings between people from different houses, such as Lupin and Tonks, Harry and Cho, and Neville and Luna. Consider your ideal romantic partner. Are they in the same house as you? What house do they belong to and why?

WEEK 30

SLYTHERIN MOMENTS:

Daily Acts of Ambition, Cunning, and Leadership

Monday

Tuesday

Wednesday

Thursday

Friday

Saturday

Sunday

WEEK 30

IMAGINE YOUR HOUSE JUST WON the House Cup.
How would you celebrate? Use this space to jot down some ideas
for the perfect House Cup party that Slytherins everywhere
would love to attend.

WEEK 31

SLYTHERIN MOMENTS:
Daily Acts of Ambition, Cunning, and Leadership

Monday

Tuesday

Wednesday

Thursday

Friday

Saturday

Sunday

WEEK 31

WHEN FIRST-YEAR HOGWARTS STUDENTS are sorted into their houses, they are only eleven years old. Do you think you would have been sorted into Slytherin when you were eleven? How have you changed or grown since then?

WEEK 32

SLYTHERIN MOMENTS:

Daily Acts of Ambition, Cunning, and Leadership

Monday

Tuesday

Wednesday

Thursday

Friday

Saturday

Sunday

WEEK 32

IN *HARRY POTTER AND THE HALF-BLOOD PRINCE*, Harry is given the task of retrieving a memory from Professor Slughorn. This poses a bit of a problem as the reluctant professor does his best to avoid Harry once he realizes what Harry's trying to do. Harry eventually solves the problem by taking a dose of Felix Felicis and appealing to Slughorn's memory of Harry's mother. As a Slytherin, how do you solve problems? When was the last time you used your Slytherin qualities to solve a problem and how?

WEEK 33

SLYTHERIN MOMENTS:

Daily Acts of Ambition, Cunning, and Leadership

Monday

Tuesday

Wednesday

Thursday

Friday

Saturday

Sunday

WEEK 33

IN *HARRY POTTER AND THE ORDER OF THE PHOENIX,*
Harry mistakenly believes a vision sent to him by Lord Voldemort that
shows his godfather, Sirius, in danger. Harry rushes to his godfather's
aid, an action that eventually leads to Sirius's death. Think about
the last time you made a mistake. Were there any aspects of
your identity as a Slytherin that played a part in the situation?
What could you have done differently?

WEEK 34

SLYTHERIN MOMENTS:

Daily Acts of Ambition, Cunning, and Leadership

Monday

Tuesday

Wednesday

Thursday

Friday

Saturday

Sunday

WEEK 34

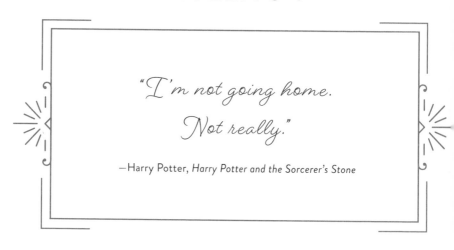

"I'm not going home. Not really."

—Harry Potter, *Harry Potter and the Sorcerer's Stone*

Everyone has special places in their lives.
Places where they feel the most like themselves. For Harry,
this is Hogwarts. Think about a space that is important to you
as a Slytherin. How does this space bring out those qualities
that symbolize your inner Slytherin?

WEEK 35

SLYTHERIN MOMENTS:
Daily Acts of Ambition, Cunning, and Leadership

Monday

Tuesday

Wednesday

Thursday

Friday

Saturday

Sunday

WEEK 35

IN *HARRY POTTER AND THE GOBLET OF FIRE*, Harry faces a Hungarian Horntail guarding a golden egg as the first task in the Triwizard Tournament. He uses his broomstick to complete the task, a decision that plays into his assets as a Gryffindor. How would you use your Slytherin qualities—cunning and resourcefulness—to achieve this task?

ABOVE: Concept art of Harry battling the Hungarian Horntail by Paul Catling.

ABOVE: More concept art of Harry and the Hungarian Horntail by Paul Catling.

WEEK 36

SLYTHERIN MOMENTS:

Daily Acts of Ambition, Cunning, and Leadership

Monday

Tuesday

Wednesday

Thursday

_____

Friday

_____

Saturday

_____

Sunday

_____

WEEK 36

IN *HARRY POTTER AND THE CHAMBER OF SECRETS*, Harry discovers he can speak Parseltongue, a skill that frightens him due to its association with Dark wizards. Have you ever discovered something about yourself that frightened you? How can you use your assets as a Slytherin to overcome that fear?

WEEK 37

SLYTHERIN MOMENTS:

Daily Acts of Ambition, Cunning, and Leadership

Monday

Tuesday

Wednesday

Thursday

_____

Friday

_____

Saturday

_____

Sunday

_____

WEEK 37

WHILE LIFE IN THE HARRY POTTER FILMS never lacks excitement, in the real world, we all get bored from time to time. But boredom can be addressed with just a little creativity. Make a list of ten things you could do right now to challenge, interest, or inspire your inner Slytherin. Refer back to this the next time you need some inspiration.

1. _____

2. _____

3. _____

4. _____

WEEK 38

Monday

Tuesday

Wednesday

Thursday

Friday

Saturday

Sunday

COLORING MEDITATIONS

Slytherin's locket is an important Slytherin artifact that is also a Horcrux. The prop in the film was based on an eighteenth-century piece of jewelry from Spain and featured a jeweled "S" on the front in diamond-cut green stones. What artifacts in your own life represent your identity as a Slytherin? Color in the locket below, and then decorate the opposite page with illustrations, taped or glued-in ephemera, or other embellishments tha symbolize these artifacts.

WEEK 39

SLYTHERIN MOMENTS:

Daily Acts of Ambition, Cunning, and Leadership

Monday

Tuesday

Wednesday

Thursday

Friday

Saturday

Sunday

WEEK 39

"For in dreams we enter a world that is entirely our own. Let him swim in the deepest ocean or glide over the highest cloud."

—Professor Dumbledore, *Harry Potter and the Prisoner of Azkaban*

Our dreams can reveal a lot about our inner world.
Write down a recent dream you had and how it
relates to your identity as a Slytherin.

WEEK 40

SLYTHERIN MOMENTS:

Daily Acts of Ambition, Cunning, and Leadership

Monday

Tuesday

Wednesday

Thursday

Friday

Saturday

Sunday

WEEK 40

IMAGINE YOU'VE BEEN MADE prefect at Hogwarts.
It's your job to help guide the new first-years in Slytherin.
Write down five pieces of advice you would give them to help
them embrace their Slytherin identity.

1. _____

_____

_____

_____

_____

_____

2. _____

_____

_____

_____

_____

_____

WEEK 41

SLYTHERIN MOMENTS:
Daily Acts of Ambition, Cunning, and Leadership

Monday

Tuesday

Wednesday

Thursday

Friday

Saturday

Sunday

WEEK 41

IN THE HARRY POTTER FILMS, Harry encounters many adult figures who he looks up to and respects—people like Remus Lupin, Minerva McGonagall, and even Severus Snape—who help shape his development into a hero. Think about a real-world Slytherin in your life who has inspired you. What about this person do you most admire and respect?

WEEK 42

SLYTHERIN MOMENTS:

Daily Acts of Ambition, Cunning, and Leadership

Monday

Tuesday

Wednesday

Thursday

Friday

Saturday

Sunday

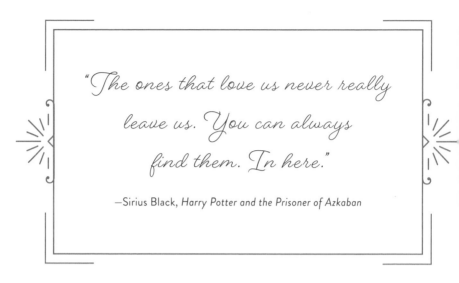

"*The ones that love us never really leave us. You can always find them. In here.*"

—Sirius Black, *Harry Potter and the Prisoner of Azkaban*

Think about someone you've lost in your life, either through death or another circumstance. Reflect on your relationship with that person and what they taught you. Did they play any part in your development as a Slytherin? How so?

_____

_____

_____

_____

_____

_____

_____

_____

WEEK 43

SLYTHERIN MOMENTS:

Daily Acts of Ambition, Cunning, and Leadership

Monday

Tuesday

Wednesday

Thursday

Friday

Saturday

Sunday

WEEK 43

THE WIZARDING WORLD IS FULL of an astonishing array of magical creatures: dragons, Hippogriffs, house-elves, centaurs, phoenixes, and more. What creature do you think embodies similar traits to those of Slytherin house? How can you bring the spirit of that creature into your daily life?

ABOVE LEFT: Concept art of a Thestral by Rob Bliss.
ABOVE RIGHT: Concept art of Fawkes the phoenix by Adam Brockbank.

CLOCKWISE FROM TOP LEFT: Concept art of Aragog in his lair by Adam Brockbank; a centaur draws his bow, also by Adam Brockbank; Harry riding Buckbeak the Hippogriff, art by Dermot Power.

WEEK 44

Monday

_____

_____

_____

_____

Tuesday

_____

_____

_____

_____

Wednesday

_____

_____

_____

_____

Thursday

Friday

Saturday

Sunday

WEEK 44

IN THE HARRY POTTER FILMS, there are moments of great danger and grief, especially in the later films as the wizarding world becomes enveloped in a devastating war against Lord Voldemort. In the real world, everyone deals with stress, pain, and emotional upheaval from time to time. That's why it's important to prioritize self-care. As a Slytherin, what does self-care mean to you? How do you take care of yourself when faced with stress or pain?

WEEK 45

Monday

Tuesday

Wednesday

Thursday

Friday

Saturday

Sunday

WEEK 45

YOU'VE JUST LANDED A MAJOR JOB INTERVIEW.
How can you use your assets as a Slytherin to get the job?
Make a list of five things you can do to prepare.

1. _____

2. _____

3. _____

_____

_____

_____

_____

_____

_____

4. _____

_____

_____

_____

_____

_____

5. _____

_____

_____

_____

_____

_____

WEEK 46

SLYTHERIN MOMENTS:

Daily Acts of Ambition, Cunning, and Leadership

Monday

Tuesday

Wednesday

Thursday

Friday

Saturday

Sunday

WEEK 46

THERE ARE SEVERAL GREAT EXAMPLES of Slytherin heroes in the Harry Potter films, the most important of which is Severus Snape. A former Death Eater, Severus Snape betrayed Voldemort in the first wizarding war and became a spy. He continues as a double agent in the second war, going to unfathomable lengths to bring about the end of the Dark Lord. Petty and even cruel, Snape is redeemed by his love for Lily Potter, and it is revealed at the end that he has been helping Harry all along. Do you consider Snape a hero? Do his actions in the war make up for his past or excuse his behavior as a teacher? What do you think defines a Slytherin hero? How can you, as a Slytherin, be a hero to someone in your life?

WEEK 47

SLYTHERIN MOMENTS:
Daily Acts of Ambition, Cunning, and Leadership

Monday

Tuesday

Wednesday

Thursday

Friday

Saturday

Sunday

WEEK 47

IN *HARRY POTTER AND THE CHAMBER OF SECRETS*,
Draco Malfoy goads Ron Weasley into attacking him by calling Hermione a
foul name, an act that plays into Ron's Gryffindor qualities of chivalry and
determination. Has anybody ever used your traits as a Slytherin against you?
How could you have handled this differently?

WEEK 48

SLYTHERIN MOMENTS:

Daily Acts of Ambition, Cunning, and Leadership

Monday

Tuesday

Wednesday

Thursday

Friday

Saturday

Sunday

WEEK 48

IN *HARRY POTTER AND THE ORDER OF THE PHOENIX*, Harry and his friends start Dumbledore's Army, a secret student group dedicated to fighting Dolores Umbridge's rules and learning practical Defense Against the Dark skills. As a Slytherin, how can you stand up for what you believe in? What kind of steps do you feel you can take to contribute?

WEEK 49

SLYTHERIN MOMENTS:

Daily Acts of Ambition, Cunning, and Leadership

Monday

Tuesday

Wednesday

Thursday

Friday

Saturday

Sunday

WEEK 49

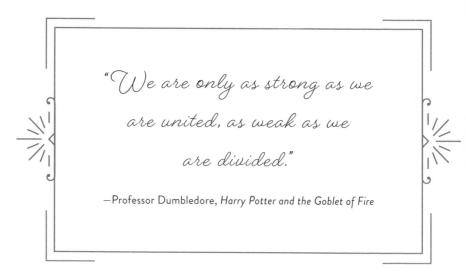

"We are only as strong as we are united, as weak as we are divided."

—Professor Dumbledore, *Harry Potter and the Goblet of Fire*

Think of a time you were in conflict with someone who embodies the characteristics of another house. How were you able to resolve the situation? Did your qualities as a Slytherin prove to be an asset or an obstacle?

WEEK 50

SLYTHERIN MOMENTS:
Daily Acts of Ambition, Cunning, and Leadership

Monday

Tuesday

Wednesday

Thursday

Friday

Saturday

Sunday

WEEK 50

AS EVERYONE KNOWS, the traits of Slytherin are ambition, cunning and leadership. After fifty weeks of reflection and cultivation, which of these traits do you identify with the most? Which do you identify with the least? Are there any additional traits that you feel match the Slytherin profile that are not talked about as much?

WEEK 51

SLYTHERIN MOMENTS:

Daily Acts of Ambition, Cunning, and Leadership

Monday

Tuesday

Wednesday

Thursday

Friday

Saturday

Sunday

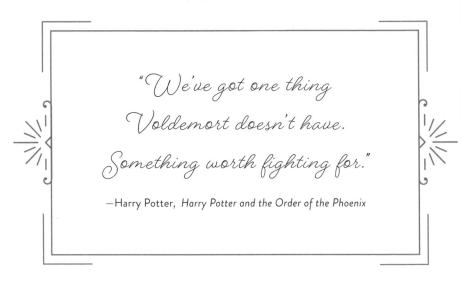

"We've got one thing
Voldemort doesn't have.
Something worth fighting for."

—Harry Potter, *Harry Potter and the Order of the Phoenix*

Everybody believes in fighting for something.

As a Slytherin, what do you think is worth fighting for?

How do you fight for it?

WEEK 52

SLYTHERIN MOMENTS:

Daily Acts of Ambition, Cunning, and Leadership

Monday

Tuesday

Wednesday

Thursday

Friday

Saturday

Sunday

WEEK 52

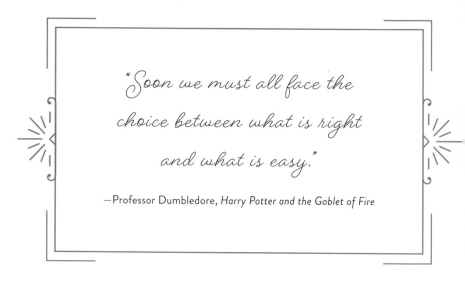

"Soon we must all face the choice between what is right and what is easy."

—Professor Dumbledore, *Harry Potter and the Goblet of Fire*

For this final prompt, reflect on what you've learned.

How do your qualities as a Slytherin help you make the right choices?

INSIGHT EDITIONS

PO Box 3088
San Rafael, CA 94912
www.insighteditions.com

Find us on Facebook: www.facebook.com/InsightEditions
Follow us on Twitter: @insighteditions

Library of Congress Cataloging-in-Publication Data available.

ISBN: 978-1-64722-236-9

Publisher: Raoul Goff
Associate Publisher: Vanessa Lopez
Creative Director: Chrissy Kwasnik
VP of Manufacturing: Alix Nicholaeff
Senior Designer: Ashley Quackenbush
Editor: Hilary VandenBroek
Editorial Assistant: Anna Wostenberg
Managing Editor: Lauren LaPera
Production Editor: Jennifer Bentham
Production Manager: Andy Harper

Text by Hilary VandenBroek

ROOTS of PEACE   REPLANTED PAPER

Insight Editions, in association with Roots of Peace, will plant two trees for each tree used in the manufacturing of this book. Roots of Peace is an internationally renowned humanitarian organization dedicated to eradicating land mines worldwide and converting war-torn lands into productive farms and wildlife habitats. Roots of Peace will plant two million fruit and nut trees in Afghanistan and provide farmers there with the skills and support necessary for sustainable land use.

Manufactured in China by Insight Editions

10 9 8 7 6 5 4 3 2